Hope is a waking dream.

~Aristotle

Also by Philip Wexler

The Sad Parade
(Adelaide Books, New York, NY, 2019)

The Burning Moustache
(Adelaide Books, New York, NY, 2020)

The Lesser Light
(Finishing Line Press, Georgetown, KY, 2022)

I Would be the Purple
(Kelsay Books, American Fork, UT, 2022)

With Something Like Hope

Philip Wexler

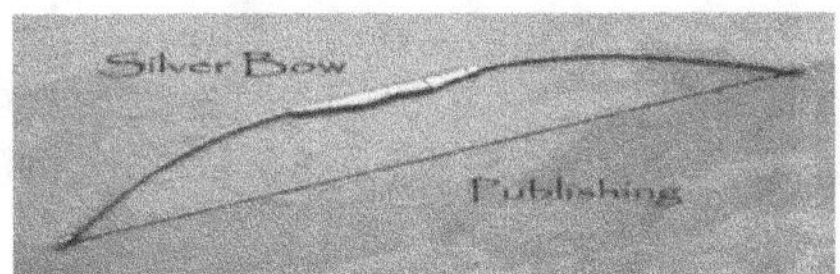

Silver Bow Publishing
720 Sixth Street, Box # 5
New Westminster, BC
CANADA   V3L3C5

Title: With Something Like Hope
Author: Philip Wexler
Cover Art: "Photo by qinghill on Unsplash"
Cover Design: Candice James
Layout and Editing: Candice James
ISBN: 9781774031858(print)
ISBN: 9781774031865 (e-book)
© 2022 Silver Bow Publishing

ISBN: 9781774032336 Print
ISBN: 9781774032343 eBook
© Silver Bow Publishing

Library and Archives Canada Cataloguing in Publication

Title: With something like hope / Philip Wexler.
Names: Wexler, Philip, 1950- author.
Description: Poems.
Identifiers: Canadiana (print) 20220406618 | Canadiana (ebook) 20220406634 | ISBN 9781774032336
   (softcover) | ISBN 9781774032343 (Kindle)
Classific\ation: LCC PS3623.E95 W58 2022 | DDC 811/.6—dc23

Dedication

For the Hope-Challenged ... Give it a Go!

CONTENTS

I.

II.

III.

I.

The true course of love never did run smooth.

~ William Shakespeare
(A Midsummer Night's Dream)

Two Crystal Goblets

Sparkling wine, endless bubbles.
Just us, at the edge of midnight,

giggling helplessly over nothing
we could put into words

or would want to. Awash
in waves of wooziness, we clink

and drink, toast giddy cheers
to a perfect future so clearly

within reach, so tangible.
We pledge eternal devotion

and succumb to dreams that,
in the end, will never be

realized or sustained,
or remembered. Poof! – gone.

Wholeheartedly, we embrace
the tenuous as if we could,

out of whole cloth create a truth
that dared not vanish or deceive.

Alarm

That he never overslept, she found
more annoying than praiseworthy.

His alarm, barely audible classical
music – a superfluous backup

because minutes before it came on,
he was awake and never drifted

back to sleep. She mocked
his *perfection*, as she called it.

He was righteously offended, proud
that he stirred awake on his own

whatever the time called for,
like clockwork, literally. She said

he had no right to lord it over her,
claimed she couldn't care less.

It didn't hit her how much
she needed his *perfection*

until he wasn't there anymore
to nudge her awake as he used to

because her shrieking buzzer
didn't help. Soon she gave up

setting her alarm, gave up
wanting to get up at all.

In the Way

In the way you shift
towards me, desiring,

or away, avoiding,
denying me, by the way

you give of yourself
wholly or piecemeal,

come without forethought
or freeze and withdraw,

I can see, as I lie,
where I stand.

In the way you sigh
or moan, artlessly

or contrived, I can hear
whether I am welcome

and should stay
or am simply in the way.

For Your Return

Comes the day
 a daisy, or scores
 of them pop open,

a wild giraffe
 gives birth
 to gangly twins

and a prospector finds
 an overlooked vein
 of silver in an old mine.

I cannot change
 and will keep
 to my calling

but stay in place
 should you decide
 to come around.

Comes the day
 the baby speaks
 its first real word,

the deadpan son
 breaks
 into laughter

and a rainbow
 rises over
 a shuttered playground.

I cannot change,
 but hold out hope
 for your return.

A Gray Reminder

Wandering the quarry,
seeking stones for a wall

to keep my memory of you
at bay, I kick up dust,

clouding the sunset,
a gray reminder

of past loss, ever
present, trouble

I might have forestalled.
Or rather, should I forego

excessive sampling and dig
my heels into this

stony place, to excavate
and sift, and maybe find

fossils of our former selves?
Here, my breath blows

gray to match the color
my hair at the temples

has begun to turn.
Light snow beginning

to fall grows sooty and old
before it hits the ground.

Truth is, I can't see myself
banishing you

from the confusion
of my dappled mind

so long as I still hear
the echo of your limpid voice,

at least not until I'm ash.
Nor should I while my heart

with all its pulsating
need finds flakes

of comfort
in your memory.

With Something Like Hope

Stuck in my spinal marrow,
the echoing residues
of last night's heated argument
and the day's silence
bend me down as I tread,
half-numb in the tail end
of afternoon, in circles,
through these dismal
April suburbs.

Only when the sun
catches up with me
at the bottom
of its downward arc
do I manage to crane
my head upwards
to see, lit from behind
and back where I started,
the shimmering crown
of the front yard crabapple,
pointillist raspberry buds
on the verge of coalescing
into a uniform cloak of color.

Put in mind of past year blooms,
and comforted the more
by the three-note song
of an unseen bird,
I straighten up and shrink
my appraisal of the argument
to proportions I can live with
as I welcome the night's descent
with something like hope.

For Better or Worse

If I could plunge into your flaming bonfire
and not be singed, but tempered by the heat,

I'd be more apt to let myself surrender,
and take on faith, your version of what's right.

I'm sick of battle, done with saving face,
and ready to give in to your designs

for love and conquest. I am not deluded.
We may get by but will never align.

This is no failing, neither yours nor mine.
I'm at your service. Here, take back your gauntlet.

Let's kiss and sign a pact of no remorse
and talk no more of guarantees, of course.

Horn of Plenty

Blessings once brimming over, cease
to endure. Destiny is fickle.

Without warning, you mock me
when I kiss the back of your hand,

a ritual you used to cherish.
Are you grown weary of courtliness

already? Overnight, it seems
our cornucopia turned

into a barely stocked tinder box
of uncertainty. Is that drooping strand

of corn silk a fuse primed to ignite?
I'm willing to risk a spark. Are you?

Rather than abundance, let's see
if we can't make sufficiency work.

It may be more than enough.
I'm ready to let the dice roll. Are you?

Sweet Nothings

Too old for the carousel's horses and the rest
of the menagerie, stationary or not, Harry and I
settled into the carriage, a robin's egg blue
overpainted with maroon streamers, swirling
green leaves, gold crowns, and pineapples,
with real spoked wheels nailed into place.

Best of all, the padded black vinyl seat
did our backsides good. Facing forward,
we had the vehicle to ourselves. I could sense
how the calliope music, our spinning,
and the breeze lifted Harry's spirits and so
my own. We needed this respite.

The Victor Herbert melody, "Kiss me Again,"
was playing when I asked him, twice actually,
because he was hard of hearing, the question
he expected of me from the days we would
ride up and down on adjacent stallions -
"Harry, are you going for the brass ring?"

The answer used to be immediate
and predictable – "Hell, yeah!" This time,
even as his eyes were rigidly fixed on mine,
he looked frail and disoriented. Struggling
for words, he patted my hand, and finally
whispered, "I found my brass ring long ago."

Touched as I was, close even, to tears,
it struck me as an odd reply, as he was miserly
with tender words. Was it a late life
stab at gallantry or was he being literal, in mind
of tangible brass rings of former times?
I didn't know and wouldn't have dared ask.

All I could do was touch his cheek and say,
"How sweet." He smiled in return.
Dizzy getting up as the carousel slowed,

he let me help him out of the carriage.
No more than guessing at the words he garbled
as he clung to me, I replied "I love you too."

Another Sad Ending

It was ages since you planted the original seeds
in that unpromising and gravelly plot you were deeded
at birth. They came up feeble as you expected,
the sprouts, shoots, mature growth, but you cultivated
the garden with the same unswerving sense of purpose
you tended to all of life's anomalies. Helpless
to determine outcomes, you grew impatient
with the infirmity of this pale, half wilted jumble
hardly reaching your ankles and so at odds
with your striving for robust fulfillment, your natural
instinct for tolerance wavered. Even then, you resisted
snuffing out totally what might yet come to fruition
for you knew that this impoverished ground
had the potential to give rise to something grand.
So, defeated and downtrodden, but determined
to salvage your one given life, you plowed
the vegetative mass under and started from scratch
the second garden that is granted to us all. This time,
against form, without preparation of the soil,
you scattered handfuls of seed, leaving them to survive
or perish. Thriving on the neglect, lush vegetation
sprung up, healthy, buoyant. You were blinded
by your quick success, and didn't take the pulse
of the land nor reckon on underlying snags, and saw
it devolve before your eyes into a sprawling tangle
of weeds and before you could grab the machete
you were entrapped and suffocated by strangler vines
bringing you to another sad ending.

A Summons to Silence

"Is it still raining?" I asked her
as she slipped into bed late
and snuggled against my body,
half-asleep and expectant.
She put a finger to my lips
as a summons to silence.

"Is it still raining?" she asked me
in her drowsiness as I loosened
myself from her body and the sheets
in the morning. Silently,
I peeked through the shutters
but pretended not to hear.

Talk

In your first few visits to my apartment
after our weekly dinner or movie or both,
you chose one of the two side chairs

and I followed suit, leaving the sofa
vacant. We spent an hour or so
with wine and talk before you primly left.

One night you settled in on the sofa,
which I took as a signal to join you there
for our conversational nightcap.

Over the weeks, the gap between us, wide
enough for my border collie happily
to fill, shrunk to a space too narrow to see.

Fingers probed. Eyes met, looked
away, met. A sip of wine now
and again. A peck here, there.

This became our holding pattern.
At best you were lukewarm
to my overtures and preferred to talk.

On the night I grew bolder and, tugging
at your arm, tried to lead you upstairs,
you disengaged and moved back to the chair.

Your breath chilled the air. I began
to apologize. You insisted we had to talk.
I said that's pretty much all we've ever done.

Thunder and Lightning

I was straining to decipher the guillotines
of water cleaving the night, the messages
encrypted in thunder and lightning,

when you strolled in, waving a receipt
over your head, babbling about being charged
for five yogurts instead of three and swearing

not to do your shopping at "that place" again.
You didn't let up until, tugging the receipt
from your hand, I said I'd leave right away

to get your money back.
You insisted on coming along
to give them a piece of your mind

but relented when I reminded you
that you'd be late for yoga. I scooped
up one of the soy vanilla yogurts

and drove through the unforgiving rain,
not to the supermarket but the lake.
There I might succeed at breaking the code

of the husky throated thunder crashing
in time to my ticking windshield wipers
dodging flashes of lightning.

I licked up the last spoonful of yogurt
just as the weather blew over but was
none the wiser about what came next.

Heading home, I wondered what excuse
you'd have for skipping yoga this time,
and checked my wallet to see

that I had two singles and change to go
with my story about how apologetic
they were at the supermarket, but there

you sat abashed, on a kitchen stool,
admitting that maybe you had bought
five yogurts after all for you found

two more at the bottom of one
of the bags you thought you had
emptied. You hoped I'd understand

that you were too distraught to go
to yoga. "Of course," I said,
"who wouldn't be?" Another round

of thunder and lightning hit the sky.
I went out to the porch to see
if I could make anything of it now.

The Ring

For years we cavorted under a steady rainbow,
growing drunk on the color that rubbed off on us,
until you asked for a ring. Flowers wouldn't do,
not anymore. Wining and dining had seen its day.
Sweet nothings were good while they lasted.
Moonlit nights listening to chamber music
on the terrace, jazz clubs or dim sum brunches,
Broadway shows, cruises on European waterways,
they were no substitute. Nor were the necklaces
and bracelets, the earrings, and brooches - not even
a close second. And the idea of it came to supplant
in your mind even our cherished rainbow.
It was a ring only, simply, no more, you wanted,
so you said – a round keepsake for your finger,
hand, heart. To me, it meant nothing, which is to say
too much. The metal, stone, carats, sparkle, expense,
may have been secondary, by your account,
but not, I could tell, negligible. All that mattered
was what it would signify to you and the rest
of the world, everything, that is, I couldn't deliver.
So, we parted ways, and the rainbow,
its visit overstayed, slowly dissipated
while the unending backdrop of sky, not showy
but more reliable, which I had lost sight of
for so long, stunned me into sobriety.

Making Allowances

It must have been due to indigestion
that she had no comment when I told her

over dessert, of the latest discovery
in my lab, bringing us one step closer

to unravelling the origins of the pandemic,
and clearly it was because the stain

wouldn't come out of her ecru blouse
that she kept interrupting as I tried

to explain that a prestigious publisher
was inviting me to write a book on my findings,

and I could only assume it was because
her best friend, Melinda, called her selfish

(one wonders why) for the first time
(to her face, that is) that she seemed oblivious

to the magazine calendar listing I shared
with her about a major museum exhibit

inspired by my research and, for certain,
I had no cause for surprise when she

abruptly hurried away from the table
the moment I mentioned my success

at being promoted to full professor since,
after all, her cell phone buzzer

interrupted us with a reminder
that she paint her toenails and, honestly,

who could blame her, after the annoyance
of misplacing her eyeglasses

for the umpteenth time, for failing
to congratulate me on being awarded

the Nobel Prize, the announcement
of which was broadcast, or so near-

strangers informed me, on the afternoon
news programs she'd tolerate now and again

as white noise when there was a lull
in the soap opera programming.

An Afternoon with Liz and Jim

On the slatted wood bench outside
McMurray's Hardware, Liz
and the baby wait, absorbed

in the finch flitting from one tree branch
to another. Unable to find the size
hanger bolts he needs, Jim rejoins them.

He is at loose ends without the hardware
to complete his project. The baby cries
when the finch disappears around a corner.

"How about," Jim says, "we drive
over to Hendrick's Tool Shed?
Maybe I'll have better luck there."

Getting up, he sees Billy Gordon
go into the Horse's Hindquarters Pub
next door.   Liz half rises with the baby

but he eases her back down
by the shoulder. "Just need a minute,
Liz, to wet my whistle."

Uneasily, she sits back down
and comforts the baby still
searching for the long lost bird.

Twenty minutes pass. She hears
Jim and Billy shouting as she expected,
and calls Eve, her sister-in-law,

who lives down the street and, unlike Liz,
is not shy about expressing her fury
She insists Liz come right over with the baby.

Walking there, Liz pictures Jim staggering
out of the Horse's Hindquarters
and fuming at her absence.

He does and is, but promptly
goes back in. He and Billy
call a truce. They commiserate

over one beer and another.
Jim couldn't care less anymore
about the hanger bolts.

On her porch, Eve and Liz
commiserate over one cup
of coffee and another.

The baby falls asleep transfixed
by Eve's two parakeets preening,
as afternoon turns to dusk.

II.

You need chaos in your soul
to give birth to a dancing star.

~Friedrich Nietzsche
(Thus Spoke Zarathustra)

Letter to his Little Brother

Hey, Jim -

Things don't seem to be going that well with you.
I caught the Internet streams the last few months.
Those shackles could not have been any fun.
I never quite got why they shaved your head
and pubic regions and they shouldn't be
broadcasting this kind of stuff but I know
you're not one to be bitter or hold a grudge.
Personally, I'd be none too happy confined
to that cage they've got you in. Anyway,
wanted to let you know your big brother
is thinking of you, and hoping things brighten
up. You've had a long haul, that's for sure.
I can't make out the language in the letter
that came with the parcel this morning
but it's postmarked the last city where you wrote
from, so I figure it's worth a shot to try
to reach you at the return address. As for
your reference to the ashes in the plastic bag
being human remains ... jokes like that
I can do without. Come on, brother, drop me
a line. Take heart. They're bound to set you
free before you know it. Just keep cool.

- Jerry

As Darkness Falls

Daylight reveals nothing
I don't already know
too well, so why bother
digging deeper?

Mechanically, I play
the cards I've been dealt
from the deck stacked
in favor of the person

I should have been.
When they blur,
I toss my hand.
Night is no less

a gamble. I shut down
in darkness, afraid
of seeing not too little
but too much.

What's hidden
is crystal clear –
where I'm headed,
when I'll fall.

The Answers

I told my father
I would do better,
but he saw through me.

I let my mother down
too many times to count.
She never got over it.

I was a model
of composure when
I needed to struggle.

I was laid back
when I needed to be
diligent.

The grief of others
bounced off me.
I tended to my own

affairs. The rest
was a distraction.
I couldn't be bothered.

I infuriated my wife
by lording
over her

My son, I left
alienated. We lost track
of each other.

I turned my back
on my friends.
They returned the favor.

I was convinced I had all
the answers. They came
back to haunt me.

The Final Beginning

You've had your share -
the ones that go nowhere,
the aborted, the stillborn,

the faltering that take
unsteady baby steps
to an early end, an impasse,

roadblock, fatigue,
collapse, or even the few
that, fooling the bookmakers,

pick up steam,
appear to be
making inroads

before detouring
off path or cliff,
or maybe

toward the conclusion
you were dreading
but here, now, this

will be the final beginning,
regardless of where it leads
or how unlikely

the outcome because, for all
your patience, you don't have
it in you to start again.

Rat Race

I used to be one of those
movers who went

up and down in brass elevators,
held sway in board rooms,

a shaker who rattled
the status quo, or so

the consensus went,
until I realized

I was a cog at best.
I had to get out

because I had nothing
left inside. For all

my wiggling and wriggling,
I couldn't budge,

tethered as I was
to conference tables,

glaring lights, droning
voices and digital miasma.

From nowhere,
a lightning storm

touched down, severed
power, connections,

leaving me electroshocked,
like a research animal.

I waited, all tremors, in the dark,
for providence, deliverance

for I knew not what.
Although I knew enough not

to expect miracles, even
with lights flickering back

to life. I'd seen too much
in the dark, of the dark,

to believe anymore
that I'd find a way out

or that one existed.
Nor could I believe

I'd ever be believable
again. Then, in the flick

of an eye – humming,
buzzing around me

and I was limply restored
but not to myself.

Shook up, too numb
to move, I sink

into inertia, wanting
nothing more.

The Last Good Day

I can't help but remember
the day fondly, not for itself
but because it assumed
a treasured patina contrasted

with the subsequent years
of days. I wake at 6, as always,
without an alarm. I let my dog,
Mr. Fluff, out in the backyard

while I put in my hour
of workout – floor exercise,
weights, stationary bike.
A quick shower is followed

by tea, cereal, and newspaper,
which I finish reading stretched
out on the sofa. Violence here,
there, everywhere, political intrigue

and nonsense, shenanigans
of the rich and famous, the expected
and unexpected. The noise
of the hospital annex construction

starts on cue as I take Mr. Fluff
for our mid-morning constitutional.
Mrs. Flint, done with weeks
of cloistered mourning for Irma

her beloved greyhound, surfaces
with Elsie, a floppy-eared Jack Russell
puppy. The dogs size each other up
without consequence. Irma and I

make canine small talk. We continue
on opposite routes and I construct
a mental list of what I want
to accomplish the rest of the day.

A steady and tiresome drizzle gives way
to unambiguous sun, no doubt
confounding the forecasters
who predicted an obstinately dismal day.

Back home, I spend too much time
paying a stack of bills, working
on my taxes, setting up a new computer
printer. This is retirement.

A lunch of bread, cheese,
and grapes. Simple. I like simple.
A nap for Mr. Fluff and me, brief
and invigorating, speaking for myself.

Back out, by bicycle, to the park.
I am grateful the three miles
is uphill. It makes the return a breeze.
I pick up where I left off

on the pen and ink sketch of the wild
persimmon. I am still unsatisfied,
wishing I was comfortable in a medium
more colorful and forgiving.

I stop at the restored grist mill
and stare absent mindedly
at the water wheel going around.
At the diner, shrimp salad,

a glass of white wine, and another.
I coast home. It's only 7.
I answer e-mails, watch
a documentary on black holes,

and call my dearest aunt in Miami
to see how she's doing three months
into chemotherapy. "Could be better."
I tell her I look forward to seeing her

in the summer as planned. I turn
to the weather channel where
they confidently announce
that tomorrow will be sunny.

Who knows what to believe?
I put my faith, instead, in Chopin,
listening to his nocturnes
before turning in. And that was it.

An uneventful day, but good.
I never ask for more. At 2 AM,
it's my aunt on the phone again.
I tell her I'll take a flight down

tomorrow. Tossing and turning,
I feel pressure in my chest, go to
the liquor cabinet with Mr. Fluff
trotting behind, and pour myself

some brandy. We fall back asleep
on the sofa. Thunder followed
by the doorbell wakes us, unless
the ringing is just in my ears.

Looking out the window, I see
someone I was not expecting
or is it me reflected in the still
dark glass? My thirst

for another drink is quashed
by a flash of lightning and more
insistent ringing. "I'm coming,"
I yell, as Mr. Fluff and I scramble

instead, for the bedroom. We close
ourselves in and he scurries
under the bed. More ringing, lightning,
and a downpour that has yet to let up.

Five Twigs on a Boulder

Routine walk. Familiar terrain
except for that boulder, new

to my eyes. Must have been
there for ages. Flat and smooth

on top as if planed, and damp
from yesterday's rain.

Five dry twigs on the surface,
like the remains of a game

of pick-up sticks. Did someone
deposit them or was it the wind?

Two are parallel and near
each other, with a third crossing

on top at an angle, forming
the mathematical symbol,

not equal to. To their right, two
overlapping, shaped like an *X*,

the endpoint of an equation
without a beginning, suggesting

that something, unspecified,
is not equal to *X*. It's not

my practice, but this time
I'm drawn to speculation,

consider how I might construct
meaning from thin air, or alter

it to fit my mood. Moving
the top twig of the *not equal to*

group to the left, and setting
it back down perpendicular

to the two remaining I create
an *I*, as in *myself*, leaving

an *equal* sign in the middle.
Thus, *I* am now equal to *X*,

a reasonable proposition since
to say I am unknown, or anything

for that matter, is not farfetched.
I leave this new rendition

for others to puzzle over
or for the wind to assimilate

into the myriad of twigs
littering the ground,

to become a kind of invisibility,
as I revert to my own.

To the Wind

My devotion steady
        as you pummel
my chest.

Panting,
        I hold my ground,
swear allegiance,

accede to your whims,
        puff up,
filling with your breath

and spinning
        like a turbine
spawning gusts

of my own,
        giving
as good as I get,

prepared for
        and wanting
more.

No Picnic

I escape
        my self-
                confinement

and decamp
        to the old growth
                pine forest

with bread,
        cheese, an apple,
                and red wine.

Deer poke their heads
        out from behind
                weathered trunks.

The stream is heavy
        with gushing
                and swirls.

A terraced rock outcropping
        serves as both
                table and chair.

I pop the cork
        and set my lunch
                on a towel.

My ancient friend, the forest
        hermit climbs out
                of the creek bed.
I invite him
        to join me.
                He takes a swig

from the bottle
        and starts nibbling
                on the food.

He has counted the pine needles
        that dropped
                this season -

3 billion exactly.
        I say it isn't possible;
                it couldn't be

so round a figure.
        He concedes
                he could be off

50,000 or so either way,
        says I am welcome
                to recount.

I roll up my sleeves,
        get down on my hands
                and knees

and start. He finishes
        my lunch and settles in
                for a nap underneath

a pine tree, his fingers twined
        behind his head,
                enjoining me

to wake him
        when I'm done
                so we can compare

notes. I want to ask the hermit
        how to tell apart
                this year's needles

from the rest
        and to delimit the boundaries
                of the count

but he is already snoring.
          The next thing I know
                    strong winds

set the trees shaking
          and displace
                    the forest litter.

With the disturbance over,
          he is gone and I reckon
                    myself absolved

from completing
          the count.
                    I retreat

to Dinah's Kitchen
          for a decent meal
                    at a corner table

where I hope not
          to be interrupted
                    as I eat and watch

from the pine porch
          an endless array of stars
                    perforating the sky.

The Inevitability of Sound

Incessant noise,
clattering, jabbering.
Wherever I turn,

my nerves are frayed.
Senseless sounds.
My jaws clench,

ears swell. No blessed
way to cancel
the infernal racket.

Even your voice,
once dulcet
and comforting,

has become another
nuisance in the earthly
chatter I cannot bear.

The droning, squeaks,
squeals, booms, bangs,
and superfluous prattle

have been unleashed,
bursting through doors,
seeping through walls.

I escape deep
into the chambers
of a forgotten cavern

beyond the screeching
bats and drip, drop, plop, splash
of water, a refuge unpeopled,

undisturbed, and wonder
if it's real. Not a peep.
Before I can catch myself,

I bellow wildly in celebration.
The pounding echo won't stop
reverberating in my head.

My Story

It's not the unique story I wish it were
but a quotidian one of bright beginnings

whose luster tarnishes in the brume
of time. A tale of unsteady footsteps,

lost bearings, off-targets, motion
without progression, of milestones

forgotten, or not memorable
or nonexistent, except for the inviting

chasms where I lie down on my right side,
desperate to come to terms with myself,

only to fall asleep, and wake up
on my left, dusty and clueless

about the inscrutable in between,
and take up where I left off, no wiser.

No sign posts. There never were. Years
I hadn't recognized as passing, finally

double me over with a combined punch
but I'm not done yet. The story lingers

as the road dips down and curves
out of sight, no destination on my radar.

Not blind to the endgame, I'm grateful
it keeps finality at bay until, without warning,

it no longer can. I beg forgiveness of my aborted
future for not holding out long enough

to live up to my expectations,
indecipherable though they were.

Wisdom in Pain

My spine misaligns
as I creep in the line.

But I've come too far
to return to my car.

I dare not shift
lest my tail bone drifts

down to my shin
and out of my skin.

I'm afraid, in the end,
I'll never mend.

My quadriceps screech
as I sluggishly reach

my fount of desire.
As neurons misfire,

my vision grown dim.
The prognosis is grim.

Getting to the head,
it seems I've been misled

or that's what they said
as I listened with dread.

I'm in the wrong line,
warned not to whine.

To double the terror,
an even worse error -

I'm in the wrong room
thus, sealing my doom.

This tragic mistake
heightens my ache.

I drag my carcass next door,
almost drop to the floor,

seeing lines without end,
I cannot unbend.

At the verge of collapse,
I hear strains of taps

but refuse to give up.
Take a drink – Bottoms up!

I shall not complain.
There is wisdom in pain.

Findings

Twice, thunder woke me last night.
The wall opposite the foot of my bed

flashed with lightning. At breakfast,
over a stale croissant that does not pair

well with the citrusy Earl Grey tea,
I notice, outside the kitchen window,

branches scattered across the yard.
Even when I head for my car

an hour later, the pavement is still soaked
and clouds are drifting away in the distance.

Sparrows on the crabapple tree zealously
shake drops of water from their wings,

chirp in complaint of what they endured
and in thanks to its passing. Waiting

for my departure, they eye the sunflower
seed feeder. The storm must have disrupted

a nest because I see, lodged between
my front tire and the curb, and shaped

like a backward S, the form
of a bird, newborn and newly dead

or perhaps the fetal remains of a lost,
shattered egg. I bend down

for a closer look at the opaqueness
of its outsized gray eyes, sightless,

overwhelming a stone silent face.
Its body is a dirty watercolor of pale

yellow, pink, and purple. I consider
running back inside to get a rag, scoop

it up, give it a modest burial. As it is,
though, I am running late for a meeting

and must hurry. That's my excuse
for skipping the ceremony, though

I have, at least, the decency
not to drive off before

dislodging the bird from the tire
with the flick of a twig

from the storm debris. As I pull
out, so does the neighborhood's stray

orange tabby from underneath
the van parked across the street.

With no pressing engagements
of its own, the cat is free

to roam wherever its heart
and hunger desires and it seemed

to know exactly where that would be
and what it would find.

Definitely

You are welcome
to listen or stop up
your ears. I've no stake
in the game.

I am here or there,
one or the other,
where I belong
or long to be.

I am sure, assured,
of how little I know
of what will come
of what I'll become.

Too many days
I've spent, misspent,
misguided, divided,
pent up, unrepentant.

But look, I'll pay
for what I've broken,
for goods I've stolen
and having misspoken,

for being mistaken,
and not conceding
that I'm lost, forsaken.
Accept my apologies

for roaming too far
while glued in place
and living, apart
from you, together,

and for everything
I've ogled or blinded
my eyes to. Though
I mingle with sin

without regret,
I never forget to seek
absolution - the best
of both worlds.

By choice, I'm trapped
where I've fallen,
willingly stuck
in between.

I've found my calling.
You won't catch me
crawling out of my zone
because too many ways

out are worse than too few.
I rest secure in being sure
of less and less of the little
left. I've no more to give

and nothing to show.
The more I consider,
the less I know.
so why are you here?

Just leave me, go.

Redemption

Here, I am
        misspent again,
        shaky, struggling,

resigned to my life
        dissipating within
        and without

until I remember
        the handful
        of seeds

I set aside
        to salvage
        the cause.

I gather the courage
        to rake
        my soul

and set them down
        with a whispered
        prayer.

Scant moisture
        from my breath
        and faint light

reflected from
        my heavy eyes
        is the most nurture

I can afford before passing
        out, but not
        for good.

I'm kickstarted
        by germination,
        propped up,

restored
        to a semblance
        of what I was

or could have been
        in better days.
        I rise, repaid,

repaired just enough
        redeemed,
        so long

as my garden
        survives,
        but should

my lifeline
        wither and wilt,
        and barren earth

unhinge my resolve
        again, still I won't
        be at the mercy

of free fall
        for always
        I'll reserve

a few spare seeds
        to see me
        through.

Moonfish Waters

Swimming like a silent bear,
I persuade the fish glowing
underwater with the sun-
borrowed light of the moon
that I am their cousin,
and so I am, no matter
that I will devour the ones
that don't escape my grip,
to save myself
as preservation
must triumph over
love and truth for all
but the noblest,
which title I can't claim,
nor will I shirk from being
picked apart myself
down to the bones
to solidify our kinship.
Let sharks approach
for they've a stake
in our eternal game.
I shall not flee
but welcome
merging with the sea.

Approximations and Deviations

This insatiable need to capture images,
sounds, experience, to scribble notes,
make sketches, gather audio, video,
evidence, to digitize, archive, because
we know no blessed other way to preserve
the meaningful, the remarkable ... alright,
even the trivial, in some single permafrost
of recollection. And all this, imperfect
though it is to restore an expired frame
of mind, allows us at least to scoop up
grains of memory, as an aid, to create
a semblance, a replacement, for what's past.
But sometimes we come closer to essences,
at least to feeling what we felt, by coloring,
knowingly or not, our perception of the truth,
or even creating from whole cloth a fiction
to substitute, to pass for what might
have been, a version as good, if good
at all it was, or better.

Collecting Mistakes

The tragedy of their going
to waste, forgotten, unheeded.
      I should have been more
      careful, must gather them

back together. I'm racking up
where I've gone wrong, what
      I've neglected, forfeited,
      just missed, the oversights.

The cache is large but most
were honest. I need them back
      as models, as spares,
      a back-pocket first-aid kit.

The thing is, I have no way
to catalog, organize them.
      Each is unique
      and bears no relation

to the rest or so I tell myself.
The best I can do is keep them
      lined up in a mental row,
      chronologically, hoping

they'll last, stay in view,
and that I can pluck out one
      or another as needed.
      My mistakes may be legion

but I can't help fearing I may
not have enough to get me through
      the worst times and
      I'll run short. From then on

I'd be destined for perfection,
infallibility, too dismal a prospect.
      How about you give me yours.
      I'll make room.

Post-Retirement

The old boss stopped by the office a couple
of times a year, as promised, to keep
in touch. By degrees, he grew haggard
and stooped, his hair thinner. Flaking

purple blotches blossomed on his cheeks.
In his heyday, he was a gushing dispenser
of handshakes and hugs, interjecting
momentary joy into the tedious workday.

As the mood struck, athletic and fit,
he'd cartwheel up and down the halls,
his thick black hair tumbling in arcs, eyes
and smile shining with mischief until the day

he retired, not quite of an age yet, but to nurse
an ailing wife. For all his good humor,
he revealed little about his private life,
and it was news to us that he was married.

After a year went by without a visit,
his name surfaced in an obituary
circulated by a co-worker and prefaced
by the words, *survived by her husband*.

I thought of writing with condolences
but was consumed by my own affairs.
My wife just left me and I'll be retiring
in a month. I won't be cartwheeling,

even in my mind, anytime soon
but maybe after everything settles down,
I'll get back in touch with the boss
and we can compare notes, so to speak.

Curbside

On either side of the flagstone walkway
where it meets the road - two spaniels,

concrete garden statuary, a patchwork
of moss covering their backs and flanks,

their muzzles smiling or maybe grimacing,
carry baskets of rock-hard grey flowers.

Forever, they've stood guard at the curb
in front of a house as forgettable as all

the others in the neighborhood. Though
in no condition to hurry toward me

with wagging tails as I approach, they are
quietly welcoming. My sounding board,

they listen impassively as I silently reveal
my innermost thoughts. For good reason,

they don't reply so I try to impose meaning
on what I take for signs, such as a shift

in the wind, a passing drizzle, or leaves
landing at their feet. In this way, I'm able

to make heads and tails of the advice
these models of canine behavior are doing

their best to impart to me. As often as not,
I leave empty-handed but they are entitled

to off-days. Their bodies have grown
dark and pitted over time, the bouquets

resembling fossilized loaves of bread.
One morning, to top off the baskets,

I gather fresh daisies from my yard,
to lend them, and myself perhaps,

some life. I look around to be sure no one
is looking, and give them each a pat.

Good Fortune

Count no man happy until he be dead. – Solon

Friends for a lifetime betray
          in an instant.
Blue chip stocks soaring upward
          for decades,
nosedive overnight
          while treasured possessions
are repossessed.
          And the love
that seemed ironclad,
          everlasting,
finally fizzles.
          Robust health is undermined
by natural decay
          or genetics
or the stars.
          The mind falters,
fades, fails.
          The pendulum ascends
only so high
          before the inevitable.
No sense rushing to revel
          in victory.
Better to reserve judgment
          for judgment day.
Yet all is not hopeless.
          Consider cases that work
in reverse when, at the end
          of the road
a downward spiraling life
          is saved in the clutch.
On this you must bank.

habitat

no choice
but birth

no escape
but death

no wish
for either

but neither
regret

a house
of cards

fragile
flattened

with a flick
rebuilt

out of habit
not need.

The Consolation of Connection

She might loll about her doorway
or go so far as to painfully stoop

an already stooping old body
to pluck a weed from the yard.

But this time, returning from a grocery
run, I see her shuffling slowly,

in a raggedy thin housecoat, down
the street. "Out for a stroll, Lois?"

"To Mrs. Fablon's," she heaves,
and points to the ramshackle house

with the steep concrete stairs
three doors down, "she can't

put the drops in her eyes no more
so, I do it for her." I hadn't seen

Mrs. Fablon, Lois's age, give or take,
outside her own house, in months.

Lois wishes me a nice day
and struggles on. I don't watch

to see how in the world
she manages the steps.

I climb my own, careful
not to exert my bad knee,

unlike the days I'd bound up
without a second thought

and wondered where, in ten years
or five or less, I might be? Would I

venture out to help a neighbor or
vice versa even if my assistance

were nominal or would we keep
to our superannuated selves?

What will I be left with by then?
Not to mention Lois and Mrs. Fablon.

Someday

Sooner or later,
if you're lucky

and prepared,
an opportunity

to take flight
will arise,

exciting you
with dreams

of migration
no less ambitious

than the Arctic
Tern's from pole

to pole.
You'll discover

the gate unlocked
and encouraged

to take your leave.
You'll be wary

of the freedom,
but tempted.

It will unsettle you
not to be held

in check anymore,
to be told you served

your time, and might
as well move on,

advised to take
advantage

of the opening.
And maybe, in disguise,

you'll do just that,
hesitant about how

you'll fit in
and worried

about the reception
that awaits you.

But if you're recognized,
welcomed, taken in,

no more than that,
you'll swear never

to leave, no matter
what someday may bring.

So Far, So Good

If you've made it
        this far,
you've come close
        enough,
thwarted the bookmakers,
        pulled it off,
and fooled the scoffers
        into believing you
earned that patina
        of legitimacy.

So, the question remains
        whether to go
the extra mile,
        risk being
unmasked of the false
        front
for the sake of proving
        to yourself
you can attain
        the very goal

you pretend
        to have already
under your belt.
        But by waiting
and debating
        long enough,
you reach your decision
        by default.
And who could fault
        you for that?

III.

Poetry involves the mysteries of the irrational
perceived through rational words.

~ Vladimir Nabokov.

Amusing Baby

Mommy covers the drinking
glass with a salad plate, sets
a salt shaker on top, inverts
a juice tumbler over it
and crowns the assemblage
with a maple syrup jar.
Baby is transfixed, stretches

unsuccessfully to grab
the place mat under it all
as mommy wags her finger,
says *no*. She pulls the highchair
away from the table and plugs
a pacifier in baby's mouth
to counteract the bawling.

I put down the newspaper
and swagger to the table.
After encasing the syrup jar
with a soup bowl as a finishing
touch, I show baby how
it's done and swiftly tug
at the place mat. It all comes

crashing down. My breathless
laughter is quickly extinguished
as mommy pops the pacifier
out of baby's mouth, stuffs it
it into mine, and fastens a bib
around my neck. Baby chortles
and claps with delight at the whole

dang spectacle. Sarcastically,
Mommy asks whether I want
the booster seat too. I go *ga ga
goo goo*. She eyes me sternly
and says she's had it up to here,
pointing to her neck, with me
and my shenanigans. Baby crawls

up on my recliner, dons my bifocals
and gazes with dismay at the Gold
Futures chart on the page I left open
in the Wall Street Journal moments
ago, its resemblance to my latest
deteriorating brain scan likely
what sparked this day's folly.

Mommy takes pity on me as I drool,
dribble, cry. She wipes my face
dry, sings me a lullaby and screams
at baby to *put down that paper
for God's sake and change Daddy's diaper
or he'll throw a tantrum and then
there'll really be hell to pay.*

.

Incident at a London Hotel

In the breakfast room, the daft white-haired gent
transfixed by the soccer match on the tube, or
at least by the visuals, strained, one could tell,
to hear the announcer. He asked every new guest
passing by, whether Adelaide was two hours ahead
of us. The people who didn't ignore him, pleaded
ignorance. Of course, with the blaring volume
of the game not registering, it was doubtful
he could hear a word anyone else ventured. Now
and then, he'd exclaim to no one in particular
that he'd be forced to go to the kitchen to see
if the chef knew, but he didn't budge from his spot.
No expert in world time zones, I shouted into his ear
that I doubted two hours was correct since I knew
we were five hours ahead of New York. He seemed
not to catch my drift and swatted me away.

With his eyes glued to the screen, he began babbling
about his lately concluded world tour - Dublin, Paris,
Rome, Nairobi, Egypt, Poland, China, and so on,
and how he could kick himself for skipping Australia -
something about his eyes giving out. "I'm retired,
you see," he confessed, as if that explained the down-
under omission. The soccer fans were cheering up
a storm. "Leave him," he bellowed at the screen, pounding
at the table and setting his empty plate and cup clattering,
"he's not worth your little finger." Noticing his gray suit jacket
on the floor as I finished my porridge and rose from the table,
I gently draped it across his chair back. Screaming
even more loudly right in his face, I told him
that if I learned any more about the time
difference between London and Adelaide,
he'd be the first to know. "You've got a brain
on your shoulders, laddie," he said. I took
a quick glance at the tube and saw, in bold letters
on a ribbon at the bottom of the screen, both London
and Adelaide time, along with the game's score
and, on the floor, a pair of eyeglasses, which must

have slipped out of his jacket pocket when it fell.

He turned his face away from the game, quite
pleased as I held them out to him. "Aha," he said,
maybe now this blasted soap opera will make sense."

His Missing Masterpiece

If Marc Chagall were alive, I'd implore
him, deplete my savings, take out a loan,

go into debt, do whatever it took,
to commission him to paint

a young couple in colorful peasant garb,
the man grabbing onto the tip of a windmill

blade and the woman clutching his free hand,
looking at each other tenderly as they spin.

The clockwise movement would be palpable,
wind visibly blowing their hair and clothing,

the man's red scarf partially obscuring
his left cheek, his eyebrows raised

in surprise and exhilaration at being there,
the woman smiling ecstatically

at their wondrous flight, and reaching
for the strings of her red and white

checkered bonnet to keep it from flying off.
The oversized gray head of a cat looks

out the windmill's lower window
and a cow with a bell around its neck

watches from the open top of a barnyard
door. A festive village bazaar filled

with dancing townspeople and musicians
permeates the surrounding field –

red, yellow, and blue predominating.
Chagall must have known he was born

to paint this scene but somehow never
got around to it. I don't begrudge him

this lapse. I get distracted myself
at moments. But what I wouldn't give

to watch him in his studio deftly
maneuvering brushes and palette,

as the canvas comes to life, and to behold
the finished creation, *Lovers on a Windmill*,

and what better title. Though mine by purchase,
ownership wouldn't be my goal, rather to have it

widely seen and appreciated so, sometime
well before I'm dead and gone, I'd set it free,

looking only to recoup my investment.
Over the years, it would accumulate

a distinguished provenance, moving
among respected dealers, galleries,

and collectors, ultimately finding its way
to a world-class museum like the Guggenheim

where it could hang prominently next to,
say, Chagall's own *Green Violinist*,

accompanied, if I'm not asking too much,
by an inconspicuous note acknowledging

my humble role in bringing *Lovers on a Windmill*,
his missing masterpiece, to light.

Ad for a Digital Device Age

Broken mop for sale, nicknamed Gladys.
        Won't squish water anymore.
It's the kind that, after you mop up,
        you push down on the handle
mechanism and it folds the sponge
        in half so you can squeeze away
the dirty water into a waiting bucket.
        You pull back up on the handle
and it's ready to moisten in order to sop up
        the next round of dirt.
Problem is, Gladys is stuck in the squeezed
        position. As to the cause -
operational failure due to metal fatigue
        is my best guess. In fact,
the sponge clamp is only partially connected
        to the wooden rod because
two of the seven proprietary screws
        have gone missing. But look,
if you're handy, there's always a work-around.
        Gladys and I have been through a lot.
I don't want to exaggerate and say
        we've been inseparable but
our relationship is far from casual.
        Also, the sponge itself is starting
to crumble but, believe me, the old girl
        has some life in her yet.
Purchased her for $20 but she is more
        of a vintage by now. Will take best offer.
Money back guarantee of course.
        And as for my reason to sell,
it's got nothing to do
        with Gladys' condition. I am moving up
to a self-propelled robotic sponge
        using state-of-the art prosthetic and drone
technologies. Please understand
        I hate to part from Gladys but
she's ever so jealous, and with
        another cleaning machine in the house,

I'd never hear the end of it.
          You'd be doing both of us
an immeasurable favor. And please,
          don't hold it against me
that I'm a cyborg. I still have feelings.

"Exceptional Service Since 1950"

It made me feel like a veritable antique,
the unremarkable phrase on the side
of the McLaughlin Electric Company's
white van, revealing to all the world,
not least of all myself, the year I was born.

Used to be, firms with a pedigree
would trot out a sign on vehicle
or storefront dating themselves
to 1879, say, or 1925, thus announcing
they were well established, venerable,

in it for the long run, no flashes
in the pan. Meanwhile, here is McLaughlin
sending electricians to fix faulty wiring,
install alarm systems, sockets, circuits.
All well and good, I'm sure, and who am I

to question their quality of service,
but to brag about going back to 1950?
You'd think it hinted at a relationship
with Thomas Edison, for God's sake.
But McLaughlin's no older than me,

putting us both firmly in the modern era ...
right? What am I, 70? It's 2020, isn't it?
Alright, I'm no youngster, but still ...
Maybe they could add "Sprightly and wise."
I suppose I should face up to the facts.

I may be getting up there in age
and forgetful of late but does broadcasting
1950 really burnish their reputation?
Alright, I'll quit griping. Here's hoping
some of their patina will rub off on me.

Stumped

Sipping tea on the sofa and looking out
the bay window, I saw a man beside a truck,
his calling card of sorts, introducing
Melvin Gleason, Tree Expert. He circled
the neighbor's massive and perfectly healthy
but lately injured oak, measuring, making notes.
A huge limb sheared off by lightning the night
before left a nasty gash. Above the crown,
a thin, wispy cloud hovered like a halo.

I knew what fate had in store for the tree,
and couldn't alter it. The Ortegas complained
about the tree blocking sunlight
in their house for as long as I'd known them.
I admired it daily, unpossessively, affectionately.
The truck was close to overflowing
with wood chip remains of other casualties.
Melvin's two partners munched sandwiches
in the cab. Vincent Ortega came out
of his house. Melvin drew his attention
to various parts of the tree. After signing papers,
they parted company, Melvin and his crew
driving off to their next job, and Vincent
and his wife to their joint law practice.

I went out to the tree and stretched to reach
its wound which I rubbed with my fingertips.
The leaves shivered as if responding to my touch.
I dug for words of consolation but could find none.
Instead, I walked around the neighborhood
seeking my own consolation from the other trees.
In the evening, back on the sofa, nursing
some brandy, I noticed the oak glowing
under a nearly full moon. Both were primed
for the day to come. Returning home,
the Ortegas turned into their garage,
their headlights sweeping my ceiling.
I drifted into a dreamless sleep. Raucous clattering

signaled morning. I could hear the truck, workers,
chain saws, woodchippers, and kids, now and again,
cheering. Behind my still closed eyes I fixated
on the stump to be and felt more helpless than ever.
I only wished the job were done already. I fell
back asleep, primed to wake to a memory.

Estate Sales

Not to be morbid, but can anyone not
be put in mind of death? Shoppers rarely ask
about the circumstances nor are they informed.
It's all about the goods, not the deceased.
Perhaps it was a woman who finally gave up
the ghost years after her husband, thus prompting
their adult children, once they'd set aside prized
possessions for family, to hire an agent
to dispose of the balance. Or maybe
it's a recently widowed man ridding
himself of his wife's belongings, cherished
by her or not, for which he has no godly use.

With everyone atwitter at the sight of reams
of stuff, why spoil the fun by calling mortality
into play. This is a time for kicking and shoving,
at making phenomenal finds, sniffing out deals,
and turning noses up at inflated prices.
People crowd in, hunting, ogling, bargaining,
charmed by vintage jewelry and clothes,
rusted tools from another era, kitchenware
with authentic nicks and stains, real paper
books with yellowed pages, torn sheet music,
banged up furniture and what, in some circles
passes for art. There's always something
for the kids who remarkably get the knack
of playing with sixty-year-old toys and games
with not a smidgen of a digital aura.

But what of that white haired woman,
richly attired, 90 if a day, an heirloom
herself, fingering one after another
of those bone china teacups and saucers,
banded in gold and patterned with roses
of burgundy, pink, and yellow? Does she stop
to consider, even for a moment, that although
a picture of health for her age, she may be next
up on that heavenly hit list, and that maybe

in a few months, if that, many of these same
restless feet will be clattering across
the floorboards of her own house and equally
grubby hands will be pawing at her own
trappings of a lifetime?

And more likely than not, just as she is doing
now, another dowager will be pulling out
a credit card, signifying her readiness to pony up
but politely asking for a discount, far from her
needing one, for this very same Royal Albert
Old Country Roses tea set because, after all,
there are only five matching saucers for the six
teacups. And how about knocking off a few
dollars more for that tiny chip
on the very tip of the pot's spout?

Room Enough

I make a circuit,
maybe several
      before I arrive
      back at *Room 1.*

Door unlocked.
Dimly lit.
      Facing me,
      slumped

in a corner,
it's myself in rags,
      legs and arms
      akimbo, unconscious

but breathing. I slap
my cheek, douse myself
      with water, carry
      myself to the cot

and smooth out
the crumpled bit of paper
      my hand is clutching.
      Room 2, it says

and, of course, I obey,
proceeding down
      the curved hallway
      to the next door

where I find
the identical situation.
      I again deliver myself
      from floor to cot

and read *Room 3*
so, I continue
      driven by fate
      and you can guess

the rest, through *Room 100*,
unoccupied, but otherwise
          looking no different
          than all the rest.

Exhausted, my knees
buckle
          and I collapse
          in a corner.

Sometime later I feel
a sting on my cheek
          and the splash
          of cold liquid.

Someone familiar
stands over me,
          escorts me
          to the cot,

examines my hands
and, disappointed
          at their flagrant
          emptiness,

seems uncertain what
to do next. We stare
          at each other.
          "Room 1?" he asks.

"I couldn't guarantee
it," I say,
          "but it's worth a try.
          Send my regards."

Happenstance

If Manuel hadn't spent an extra ten minutes
that morning 30 years ago glued to the news
of our presidential assassination,
he wouldn't have ended up on the late bus

seated next to Gabriela, whom he would marry,
a fussy baby girl on her lap. If it weren't
for Gabriela's papá, director of Banco General,
putting in a good word on his behalf,

Manuel wouldn't have been recruited
by the bank, risen up the ranks in leadership
positions and retired with accolades
as El Director himself twenty years later,

honored at that time with a posh reception
in the city conservatory. Chatting there
by chance with the horticulturist, he decided
to embark on a second career of landscape

design, ultimately becoming El Director
of the globally acclaimed Manuel Garden
Studios. This was why he was retained
to renew the palace grounds of my own papá,

our cherished presidente who assumed power
after the cold-blooded murder
of his predecessor by a masked rebel
who escaped with impunity.

And if it weren't for Manuel surveying
our grounds, I would never have chanced
to encounter him and Gabriela
in the grand allée of live oaks.

It was because my conference
with the editors of *Revista Moderna*
was postponed that I had the time
to invite the couple to the patio

for a sip of port from our vineyards,
and where I agreed to write the biography
of Manuel, to be called *El Director Excelente*.
This gave rise to my interview

with his stepdaughter, Maria, a charming
but nervous young woman
whose paranoia only emerged
after she became my wife,

and who developed a loathing
for my papá, El Presidente,
and his despotic rule, as she called it.
Thus, one day as papá joined us

for a glass of port in our gazebo,
his wedding gift to us, lavishly
constructed with public funds funneled
directly to Maria's papá, El Director,

I was relieved to discover her demeanor
restrained and cordial. With smiles all around,
I stepped away from the table to join
our young son, Miguel, watering the roses.

Hearing, in no time, loud voices, I turned
to see Maria spit in my papá's face
before touching a pistol barrel
to his forehead and firing.

Miguel dropped the watering can,
soaking my feet as if with the blood
of papá. Thus, unexpectedly,
I happened to become El Presidente.

Somewhere Down South

I was in a car on an interstate somewhere
down south, dead still in traffic, air conditioner
busted, sweating bullets, windows open,
breathless from the exhaust coating my lungs.

To my left, behind sheets of orange
tinted glass – GNAT Industries,
standing, I imagined, for Godawful
Nausea, Air Pollution, and Toxicity.

Going nowhere, I focused my binoculars
on the cubicles inside where modern
day pencil pushers sat hypnotized
by computer monitors, fingering

keyboards, cradling mice. It was the life
I was escaping. Next door, the Happy Duck
Motel with its drained outdoor pool
devoid of people, ducks, or happiness.

Across the way, Dreamy Roads
Dry Cleaning with, daylight be damned,
a glowing sign shouting, in big numbers,
"$1.99," dwarfing the fine print below -

"Most Items." Despite the coffee I was
relentlessly guzzling from my three
oversized thermoses, I was half-asleep
at the wheel. Behind me, a horn blast

infused with anger made me realize
it would be safe to accelerate to 10 mph.
A volley of thunder followed. "Yes,
that's exactly what's been missing,"

I thought. As rain swamped the asphalt,
the traffic surprisingly let up enough
for me to approach the lightning pace
of 30 mph. Down the road, more

enticements - Wise Guy Auto Parts,
Jeff and Jerry's Waffle Shack, Denise's
Outlet Heaven, and the well-timed
Welcome Center, to where, I hadn't

the faintest. I knew I wouldn't be in
for adoring fans waving and applauding
my entrance and throwing kisses.
With my thermoses drained and in dire need

of bladder release, I was willing to accept
the snub which was more than made up for
by the beckoning unisex male-female
schematics on three restroom doors.

As it turned out, storm related flooding
forced them all closed. Back on the road
with traffic stalled again and the next rest
stop 16 miles away, I found myself crawling

past Lakeside Down Home Chicken Wings
and the double-take worthy sign for Lucky
Dan's High-Tech Batter, the letters *i*, *e*, and *s*,
presumably missing from the last word

which surely must have been *Batteries*
in keeping with the huge model of a 9 volt
spinning on a pole. Unable to hold out much
longer, I pulled off, just past Lucky Dan's,

at a stand of trees I wished were denser, but
would have to do, even if it meant becoming
a roadside attraction myself, sighing in relief,
in the steamy pouring rain somewhere down south.

Albrecht Dorferhosen V of Voscovia

This 19th century master composer registered
his first symphony as Number 3, his second
as Number 6, and so on in intervals of three,
quite legally, with Voscovia's copyright office,

causing endless grief, though, for generations
of conductors, musicians, impresarios, DJs
and classical music aficionados. Albrecht
Dorferhosen V was the name given to him

by his father and recorded in his Voscovian birth
record, even though it was common knowledge
that his father, an opera baritone and weekend
chimney sweep, was Albrecht Dorferhosen II,

so that his son, logically, should have been
the third Albrecht Dorferhosen, not the fifth.
According to some, this paternal tomfoolery
may have influenced the peculiar numbering

scheme his son adopted for his musical
compositions. Indeed, the Maestro, who
conducted on the side, carried it a step further
for, whatever the number, 3, 6, 9, the fact

remained that these were not symphonies
at all. Albrecht Dorferhosen V never wrote
a symphony. They were virtually all
mandolin concertos, and unfinished at that.

The exception was his so-called Symphony
Number 26, *The Grandiose*, the only one he notated
as "unfinished," although it bore all the hallmarks
of an absolutely complete concerto.

The Maestro's eccentricities, overshadowed
by the brilliance of his music, were little
heeded during his lifetime and left
for future generations to scrutinize.

At age 50, he gave up music to write
the definitive history of Voscovia,
setting out to prove that the principality
dated back to a 76 AD Roman occupation

contrary to the generally accepted
legend of its founding in 537 by the Ostrogoths.
He struggled with the research and writing
for thirty-five years, but had completed a total

of only twelve pages when he was killed in a duel
with sharpened batons by Reinhart von Wahr,
a rival composer of note. Von Wahr claimed
that his sonata for piccolo and piano,

his only musical composition, was repeatedly
plagiarized by Albrecht Dorferhosen V.
Von Wahr sought, and found, satisfaction,
to the dismay of his victim's countless admirers.

The Maestro's widow confirmed the existence
of 312 musical scores, a far cry from the 736
he himself claimed, but certainly
of a quantity and quality to ensure

his ranking among the greatest of all
Voscovian composers. While his twelve pages
of history continue to be mined for insights,
it is as a musician that his legacy survives.

Luminaries of the musical world attended
Albrecht Dorferhosen's funeral where
a solo bassoonist played at a slow and somber
pace, the second allegretto vivace movement

of his characteristically and inaptly named
Viola Trio for Voice and Mandolin,
After the Style of Alberta Dorferhosen,
in homage to his daughter, untutored

in music though she was. Alberta was more
often addressed as Albertus, due to
her masculine persuasions. Donations financed
a bronze memorial statue for the Maestro

smack in the middle of the town square. Titled
Equestrian Monument to Musical Singularity,
it depicts him astride a leaping dolphin.
It survives to this day, oxidized, and bedecked

with graffiti and good wishes from countless
pigeons. It is the destination for scores
of adoring musical pilgrims who strew flowers
at its base under the impression that the statue

is memorializing Fraulein Flipper, the beloved
dolphin mascot of Voscovia who expired of grief
at the very moment Dorferhosen was pierced
through the heart in his ill-fated duel.

Bronx Man Working in Yard
Slain in Dispute over Broom

The cabbie pulled over to the curb.
A straw broom with a wooden shaft
was poised, bristles in the air, alongside
a trash can waiting for the day's pickup.

The homeowner, edging his lawn
saw the cabbie get out and grab it.
"Hey, bro, you takin' my broom."
"Ain't yo broom, man, it garbage."

The homeowner had set the broom
by the trash temporarily
after sweeping his flagstone steps.
He warned the cabbie that it was his,

and he'd better drop it pronto.
The cabbie said that the county
owned all the land fifteen feet in
from the curb, as if that mattered.

When the homeowner reached
for the broom, the cabbie,
with his free hand, pulled a pistol.
 "Don't you touch it or you be sorry."

That didn't prevent the homeowner
from whisking the broom away
from the loose grip of the cabbie
who proceeded to shoot his adversary

in the forehead, point blank.
The homeowner held tight
to the broom as he collapsed,
his head hitting the trash can

with a clang, adding insult to injury.
"Keep yo' stinkin' broom, man,"
said the cabbie in a momentary burst
of generosity until he realized that

his fingerprints would be evidence.
He quickly extricated the broom
from the homeowner's dying fingers
just as his wife ran out of the house

with a fearsome looking cleaver.
He tossed the broom on the back seat
of his cab, its blonde head sticking out
the driver's side window. He turned on

his meter as if he'd just picked up a fare.
Mrs. Homeowner, in tears, crumpled
on top of her husband and waved the knife
at the cabbie. He pointed to the broom.

"Ain't never gonna see this baby back, bitch.
So long." He sped off to the Atlantis Diner
where he propped the broom on the bench
across the table as if it were joining him

for a meal. Finishing his omelet
and coffee, he heard sirens.
A cop rushed in and nodded his head
in approval as he compared the broom

to a sketch in his hand. "Confirmed, Chief,"
he whispered into his phone, and then
to the cabbie, "You'll do time for this, my man.
Kidnapping a broom; how low can you stoop.

We've seen your kind before –
a little too big for your britches.
You won't be able to sweep
this one under the rug."

The Fix

The casino portion of the church's fundraiser
      done, the geriatric but well-heeled crowd
graze on the dinner's main course of a pale fish-
      like substance in a paler gelatinous sauce
partially concealing a nearby starchy mass
      that might once have been mashed potatoes.
As for the limp and slimy string beans, success
      at spearing or scooping them up with a fork
takes several tries. Most everyone is relieved
      when the waiters whisk away what remains,
which is most of what they started with, and deliver
      the dessert course. The old folks nibble
contentedly on thin, dried-out slices of carrot cake
      and sip lukewarm coffee or an analogue thereof.

After an equally tepid and seemingly spontaneous
      tapping of spoons on cups to call
for silence, the good Reverend Loki bounds
      onto the stage, accompanied
by feeble rounds of applause. He pulls
      out all the stops, proclaiming
the power of family, patriotism, straight thinking,
      clean living and, above all,
faith, to a sprinkle of amens from the half-asleep,
      reprobate flock. A few elbow-nudge
their neighbors and wink at the clean-living part.
      They know quite well what Reverend Loki
has been up to all these years and can't think
      of a holier way to be led astray.

Outside, two teenagers puncture the already
      underinflated tires of the Reverend's
motorcycle with a hypodermic syringe.
      The superannuated struggle to be attentive.
Arthritic hands clap randomly, and barely audible
      hosannas struggle to emerge from gravelly
throats. "Don't fall into the trap of complacency.
      You have the God-given gifts to fix yourself.

Use them." One out-of-place young guy in swank
          duds consults his diamond encrusted
pocket timepiece often, as does Reverend Loki
          the clock on the opposite wall,
as if they both have imminent engagements
          they cannot afford to break.

Thanks to a morning hangover, the Reverend
          has been running late all day. Now he must
hurry through his oration so he can get down to 34th
          Street and Honiker to keep his appointment
with the new dealer. He concludes with a homily
          about salvation through prayer and replies
to a few mumbled questions with unrelated stock
          answers. After deducting for miscellaneous
expenses, the cashier converts the accumulated
          donations from 15 bowls into five crisp
hundred-dollar bills, which Reverend Loki
          steals with a feel from the bosom
of the hat-check girl, before he makes for the door.
          His motorcycle tires are dead flat.

The vandals get a kick out of watching him
          from the window of the Hallelujah Ale House
just across the way. The dude with the flashy
          pocket watch catches up with Reverend Loki,
taps his shoulder, shakes his hand, and intones,
          "A very moving sermon. I am a changed man."
By now, the Reverend is badly in need of a fix
          and in no mood to socialize. "Listen, my son,"
he says, eyeing the Tesla his admirer has just unlocked
          remotely, "How about a lift downtown?"
"My pleasure, your Holiness. Anything to help."
          "Your kind deed shall be rewarded many times
over, I assure you" The Reverend slides a flask
          out of his back pocket, takes a swig and

offers it to his new-found driver, simpatico and eager
          to assist. "You wouldn't be passing
anywhere near 34th and Honiker, by chance?"

        "My very destination." his disciple replies,
removing a black velvet pouch from his pocket,
        "But why don't we do the deal right here,
Reverend? Go ahead, role up your sleeve. No need
        to stand on ceremony. And so sorry
about your motor bike. The boys misunderstood
        my orders as always. I simply told them
not to lose sight of it, as a precaution you understand.
        No worries, though. Let's just see the cash
and we'll get you fixed up." And to their ever-
        lasting credit, by God, they both delivered.